The Quangle Wangle's Hat

by Edward Lear

Licensed exclusively to Top That Publishing Ltd
Tide Mill Way, Woodbridge, Suffolk, IP12 1AP, UK
www.topthatpublishing.com
Copyright © 2013 Tide Mill Media
All rights reserved
2 4 6 8 9 7 5 3 1
Manufactured in China

Illustrated by Sam McPhillips
Written by Edward Lear

ISBN 978-1-78244-214-1

A catalogue record for this book is available from the British Library

'For my friends Matt, Hannah, Quint and Mr Hooper x'
Sam McPhillips

On the top of the Crumpetty Tree
The Quangle Wangle sat,
But his face you could not see,
On account of his Beaver Hat.

For his hat was a hundred and two feet wide,
With ribbons and bibbons on every side
And bells, and buttons, and loops, and lace,
So that nobody ever could see the face
Of the Quangle Wangle Quee.

The Quangle Wangle said
To himself on the Crumpetty Tree,
'Jam; and jelly; and bread;
Are the best of food for me!

'But the longer I live on this Crumpetty Tree,
The plainer than ever it seems to me
That very few people come this way
And that life on the whole is far from gay!'
Said the Quangle Wangle Quee.

But there came to the Crumpetty Tree,
Mr. and Mrs. Canary;
And they said, 'Did you ever see
Any spot so charmingly airy?

'May we build a nest on your lovely hat?
Mr. Quangle Wangle, grant us that!
O please let us come and build a nest
Of whatever material suits you best,
Mr. Quangle Wangle Quee!'

And besides, to the Crumpetty Tree
Came the Stork, the Duck, and the Owl;
The Snail, and the Bumble-Bee,
The Frog, and the Fimble Fowl;

(The Fimble Fowl, with a corkscrew leg;)
And all of them said, 'We humbly beg,
We may build our homes on your lovely hat,
Mr. Quangle Wangle, grant us that!
Mr. Quangle Wangle Quee!'

And the Golden Grouse came there,
And the Pobble who has no toes,
And the small Olympian bear,
And the Dong with a luminous nose.

And the Blue Baboon, who played the Flute,
And the Orient Calf from the Land of Tute,
And the Attery Squash, and the Bisky Bat,
All came and built on the lovely hat
Of the Quangle Wangle Quee.

And the Quangle Wangle said
To himself on the Crumpetty Tree,
'When all these creatures move
What a wonderful noise there'll be!'

And at night by the light of the Mulberry moon
They danced to the Flute of the Blue Baboon,
On the broad green leaves of the Crumpetty Tree,
And all were as happy as happy could be,
With the Quangle Wangle Quee.